Farm Friends!

P9-DGI-653

Blue's Clues & you!

By Mei Nakamura
Illustrated by Dave Aikins

A Random House PICTUREBACK® Book

Random House 🏠 New York

© 2023 Viacom International Inc. All Rights Reserved. Nickelodeon, Blue's Clues & You!, and all related titles, logos, and characters are trademarks of Viacom International Inc. Published in the United States by Random House Children's Books, a division of Penguin Random House LLC, 1745 Broadway, New York, NY 10019, and in Canada by Penguin Random House Canada Limited, Toronto. Pictureback, Random House, and the Random House colophon are registered trademarks of Penguin Random House LLC.
rhcbooks.com
ISBN 978-0-593-56940-5 (trade)
Printed in the United States of America
10 9 8 7 6 5 4 3 2 1

Hi there! I'm Josh. Today, Blue and I skidooed to the farm!

Blue is excited to meet lots of farm animal friends. But what else does Blue want to do on the farm? Will you play Blue's Clues with us to figure out what Blue wants to do?

Great! Now, remember: Blue's paw prints will be on the clues—Blue's Clues! We have to find all three clues. Then we'll put them in our Handy Dandy Notebook!

Our first stop at the farm is a great big pasture. I see cows and sheep munching on the grass. Hi, cows! Hi, sheep! Look at their babies!

A baby cow is called a calf. What's a baby sheep called?
Yeah, a lamb! So sweet!

Do you see a paw print? Yeah, there on the grass. Grass is our first clue. Let's put it in our Handy Dandy Notebook!

Our next stop is the old red barn. We can look for more Blue's Clues there. Let's go and see what's inside!

Before we go into the barn, let's say hello to some new farm friends with Blue. Hey there, pig and little piglet!

They're rolling in the mud to cool down. That looks fun . . . but maybe a little dirty!

There are more farm friends inside the barn!
Hello, mama horse! Hello, little foal! That looks like
some tasty hay you're eating!

What else do you see? A clue?

Oh! There's a paw print on that blanket! Let's draw it in our Handy Dandy Notebook.

So we have two clues: grass and a blanket. What could Blue want to do on the farm with grass and a blanket? Hmm. We'd better find that last clue!

Here's the chicken coop. Blue wants to say hi to the whole chicken family!

The mother hen says *cluck, cluck*. The chicks say *peep, peep*. What does the rooster say? *Cock-a-doodle-doo!*

Look! There are other birds in the pond over there. I see a duck and a little duckling swimming around. Do you see another clue, too?

Yeah! The clue is next to the duck pond on that basket full of food! We have all three clues now. Time for the Thinking . . . Hmm. We don't have our Thinking Chair here. Let's sit on the Thinking Tractor!

Let's think. What could Blue want to do at the farm with grass, a blanket, and a basket full of food?

Do you know what Blue wants to do? You do? What is it? A picnic! Yeah, Blue want to have a picnic with her new farm friends! We just figured out Blue's Clues!

What a great day for a picnic on the farm! And all our new friends came, too! *Farm*-tastic!

Thank YOU for helping me figure out Blue's Clues. You sure are smart! See you soon!